Italian Wedding Murder

Book Four

in

Papa Pacelli's

Pizzeria Series

By

Patti Benning

Author's Note: On the next page, you'll find out how to access all of my books easily, as well as locate books by best-selling author, Summer Prescott. I'd love to hear your thoughts on my books, the storylines, and anything else that you'd like to comment on – reader feedback is very important to me. Please see the following page for my publisher's contact information. If you'd like to be on her list of "folks to contact" with updates, release and sales notifications, etc...just shoot her an email and let her know. Thanks for reading!

Also...

...if you're looking for more great reads, from me and Summer, check out the Summer Prescott Publishing Book Catalog:

http://summerprescottbooks.com/book-catalog/ for some truly delicious stories.

Contact Info for Summer Prescott Publishing:

Twitter: @summerprescott1

Blog and Book Catalog: http://summerprescottbooks.com

Email: summer.prescott.cozies@gmail.com

And...look up The Summer Prescott Fan Page on Facebook – let's be friends!

If you're an author and are interested in publishing with Summer Prescott Books – please send Summer an email and she'll send you submission guidelines.

TABLE OF CONTENTS

ITALIAN WEDDING
MURDER

Book Four in Papa Pacelli's Pizzeria Series

CHAPTER ONE

"Thanks for choosing Papa Pacelli's. Have a nice day."

Eleanora Pacelli smiled as she watched the woman and her two young daughters walk away, pizza box in hand. Even after working there for months, she still enjoyed the simple things, and nothing could compare to watching yet another satisfied guest leave.

"Hey, Ms. Pacelli. Is she here yet? I heard the door open."

That was Clara, one of Ellie's employees. She was poking her head out of the kitchen door, looking eagerly around the restaurant.

"Not yet. A customer just left. I'm sure she'll be here soon, though," the pizzeria manager said.

"Let me know the second she walks in," the young woman said. "I can't wait to meet her."

The week before, Ellie had spent days interviewing potential new employees for the pizzeria. Three employees and herself just wasn't cutting it, especially not with the restaurant's increased success since she had started managing it. It had been a nerve-wracking process for her; all of her current employees had been there for longer than she had, having been hired by her grandfather before he passed, and she was anxious to find someone that would fit in well with everyone that already worked there.

After days of interviewing several applicants, Ellie was certain that she had, at last, found the perfect new employee. Still, she was worried. Even her grandfather had made a mistake once; he had hired Xavier Hurst, after all. The young man had been the worst employee possible. Not only had he let the pizzeria fall into disrepair, but he had also stolen thousands of dollars from it over the course of the two years that he had worked there. The fiasco was the perfect example of how dangerous it could be to trust the wrong people.

As the clock ticked closer to three, when the new employee was supposed to show up, Ellie began casting anxious glances out the window. It would be embarrassing if her first hire was a no-show on the very first day.

She felt a rush of relief when she finally saw a girl with brightly colored, spiky hair walking down the sidewalk towards the pizzeria. "Clara, she's here."

Her employee appeared so suddenly that Ellie got the feeling she had been waiting right by the kitchen door. "Is that her?"

"Yes." She looked over at her employee and saw a flicker of doubt cross her features. *It's the hair,* Ellie thought. *I had my doubts at first, too. But I really like her, after spending some time speaking to her.*

The young woman crossed the street and let herself into the pizzeria. Ellie smiled at her. "Hi, Iris. This is Clara Callahan, another one of my employees. She'll be handling the majority of your training today. Clara, this is Iris."

"It's so nice to meet you, Clara," Iris said. "I can't wait to get started."

"It will be nice to have someone else around," Clara replied, still eying the new girl's brightly colored hair.

"All right, follow me into the back, Iris, and I'll get you your shirt and hat. Then Clara will start showing you the ropes in the kitchen," Ellie said, still smiling. She was determined to make her new employee feel as comfortable as possible.

It didn't take long for Clara to overcome her misgivings about Iris, and soon the two young women were chatting happily in the back. Eleanora was pleased. It seemed like her first new hire had been a success. Once Iris was trained up enough to work on her own, they would all be able to take more time off. It would be easier to get another employee to come in if someone called in sick, too.

Happy to let her two employees get to know each other, Ellie spent the next few hours at the register, chatting with customers and taking orders, which she called back to Iris and Clara. She saw a lot of familiar faces; Kittiport was a small town, after all, and Papa Pacelli's had a lot of regulars. She was on the verge of taking a break when someone she knew even better than most of her customers walked in.

"Hey, Ellie," her best friend, Shannon Ward, said. "How are things going?"

"Pretty well. The new employee started today," Ellie told her. "What can I get you? I can call back the order, then take a short break and chat while you're waiting, if you want."

"Actually, I'm not here for pizza," Shannon said. A grin broke out across her face. "I'm here on business."

"Oh?" Her friend was a journalist for the local newspaper. She had a column of her own, in which she covered the multitude of miscellaneous events around town, such as the outcome of a quilting contest, or who caught the smallest fish in the fishing competition.

"My boss thought I would be the perfect person to cover this story, since we're friends. It's going to be on the front page and everything," the other woman continued.

Ellie was lost. Nothing news-worthy had happened to her or to the pizzeria for weeks — and she was happy to keep it that way.

"I don't have any idea what you're talking about, Shannon."

"The anniversary, of course," her friend replied. "What do you have planned?"

"Anniversary?" Ellie said blankly. She wasn't married. It could be her grandparents' anniversary, she supposed, but she had no idea why that would be a story worthy of the front page of the newspaper, even for such a small town.

"For Papa Pacelli's, of course. Monday will mark twenty years from the time your grandfather first opened the doors. At the ten-year anniversary, he had a big party and invited everyone. There was a raffle for a year of free pizzas — one a week for the entire year — and all of the proceeds went to charity." Shannon's face fell. "You don't have anything planned, do you?"

"Of course I do," Ellie said, struggling to come up with something on the spot. In truth, she had had no idea that the pizzeria's twentieth anniversary was approaching, let alone that she was expected to celebrate it. She couldn't send her friend away without a story, though. "I thought I'd do the same thing that my grandfather did ten years ago. Another big party, with a raffle, and some sort of pizza buffet."

"Awesome," Shannon said. "I can't wait. I'll be there early to take lots of pictures. This is going to be great publicity for both of us — my name and your restaurant, both on the front page of the newspaper. I'll make sure the whole town knows about Papa Pacelli's twentieth anniversary party!"

The pizzeria manager smiled, hoping that her friend wouldn't be able to see through the expression to the panic that lay beneath. How in the world was she supposed to plan an event for the whole town, in just three days?

CHAPTER TWO

"Twenty years already? Oh my, I can't believe it's been that long," Ann Pacelli said, putting down the apples she had been peeling and looking suddenly tired. "Twenty years ago, your grandfather would have been retiring from his job at the paper mill, and I thought we were getting old *then*. It can't really have been that long, can it?"

"Twenty years ago, I was in college. It's a long time for me too, Nonna." Ellie took over the peeling, gently encouraging the older woman to go and sit down. "So, do you have any ideas for this party I'm supposed to throw? Do you remember what Papa did last time?"

"The ideas you have already sound good to me. Maybe you should have some games, in addition to the raffle?"

"Like what?" She looked down at the apple in her hand and realized she already had one answer. Kids still enjoyed bobbing for apples, didn't they? "Nonna, do you have any old pictures of the pizzeria? I was thinking I could blow them up and hang them around the restaurant, so people could see how it's changed over the years."

"That's a wonderful idea, dear. I know I have some in one of the photo albums in your grandfather's study. We can look through them once the pies are in the oven."

Of the three apple blueberry pies they were making, only one was for the Pacelli women. The other two were going to friends of Ann's — friends that had recently gone into nursing homes. Ellie knew her grandmother was dreading the day she would become unable to care for herself. She didn't seem to quite believe her granddaughter when she promised that she would stay and care for her in their house.

It didn't take long for the two of them to put the finishing touches on the pies and get them in the oven. Ellie carried a small bowl off apple wedges and blueberries sprinkled with cinnamon out to Marlowe, her grandfather's green-winged macaw. The huge red parrot dove beak first into the dish, mashing the fresh fruit with her beak. The pizzeria manager knew that she was going to have quite the mess to clean up later — the bird was a notoriously messy eater — but Marlowe's enjoyment made it all worth it.

Leaving the macaw to her feast, she and her grandmother made their way down the hallway that lead to the sizable study. Bunny, Ellie's little black and white papillon, followed them, knowing that the big desk in the study held dog treats that were a lot tastier than the apples and berries the bird got.

"Here you go, Bunny," Ellie said, tossing a couple of cookies down onto the dog bed that she kept by the desk. Her nonna walked straight over to the shelves and began pulling down old photo albums. In no time at all, they had found more pictures of the pizzeria in its early days than she would ever need.

"Hmm. It looks like I took a lot of photos in the first couple of years, but haven't taken as many recently," the older woman said. "You know what we need? A current picture, one with you out front."

"No, Nonna, I haven't been there long enough to —"

"Nonsense. You're the reason the pizzeria is as successful as it is right now. If you hadn't been able to come and help out after your grandfather passed, well, I'm afraid I would have ended up selling it."

"Well, if you insist... but I want you to be in it, too."

With only two days left to prepare, time was of the essence. Ellie gathered her favorite of the old photos of her grandfather and the pizzeria and put them in her purse alongside the camera her grandmother handed her. What was supposed to have been a quiet Saturday morning with some light baking, was quickly becoming far busier than she had planned.

"Are you sure you want to go with me to get the pictures blown up, Nonna?" she asked as she helped her grandmother in the car. "I have no idea how long it will take. I would be happy to drop you off back here at home first."

"No, no, I'll stay with you, dear. We can take a stroll around town while we wait. I'll even treat us to lunch, if you'd like."

Their first stop was at the local nursing home, where Ellie helped her grandmother carry in the two still warm pies. After a good twenty minutes of visiting with each of her friends, Nonna, was ready to go to their next destination; Papa Pacelli's. Ellie still wasn't sure how she felt about hanging her own picture on the wall of the little restaurant. It felt a bit too much like tooting her own horn. She had really hardly done anything there, and she certainly didn't feel like she deserved a spot of honor alongside her grandfather.

Nonna quickly corralled a pedestrian and asked him to take the picture for them. Ellie posed with her arm around the older woman's shoulder, a smile on her face. It was impossible to say no to her grandmother.

They dropped the camera with the new picture on it along with the stack of old photos off at the copy shop, which promised to have them blown up to the right size in an hour. That left them with a good amount of time to walk around town and chat, something that they hadn't done as much of lately as the weather got colder.

"So, how are you settling in, Ellie?" Nonna asked, linking her arm with her granddaughter's. The old woman's pace was slow, and Ellie was once more reminded that her grandmother wasn't as young as she acted sometimes — she was well into her eighties.

"I think I'm settling in pretty well, Nonna. I'm definitely getting used to running the pizzeria."

"I don't mean just as far as business goes. How are *you?* Are you happy here? Are you making friends? Have you gone on any more dates with that sheriff?"

"No, like I told you, that was just a one-time thing," she told her grandmother gently. She had explained to the older woman before that the only reason for their dinner date had been to help solve a case; there had been no romance involved. Nonna, however, remained convinced otherwise.

"You two went so nicely together, dear. I really think you should give him another chance."

"Nonna..." Ellie sighed. She knew it was no use arguing with her grandmother. "I promise, if he asks me to go on a date with him, I'll say yes." *There*, she thought, *that should do it. I'm not lying to her, but since he's never going to ask me out, I won't ever have to follow through.*

"Wonderful," Nonna said, brightening up. "Now, I promised you lunch, didn't I? Where would you like to eat?"

"Um, I'm not sure." She looked around, hoping for inspiration. They were right across the street from Cheesaroni Calzones; Papa

Pacelli's main competitor. Her grandmother saw it at the same time she did. They met each other's eyes, and Ellie gave a snort of laughter. "Anywhere but there. You choose, Nonna. And I'll pay. You do enough as it is."

CHAPTER THREE

It wasn't easy, preparing for the party over the weekend, but somehow Ellie managed it. She thought the pizzeria looked very good when it opened Monday afternoon. Iris, Rose, and Jacob, who had all agreed to come in early and help out, had spent a few hours in the morning shopping at the local party store. Now black and red streamers — to match the restaurant's wall tiles and paint — were hanging from the ceiling. Balloons had been blown up and put outside, and a big banner that read *Happy 20th Birthday!* was hanging over the register. All in all, it was very reminiscent of their grand re-opening party, in which Papa Pacelli's had turned over a new leaf.

The main differences were the raffle — fifty-two weeks' worth of free pizzas — and the buffet table. Just a few dollars would get each guest unlimited pizza. They were bound to take a financial loss on the day, especially since the proceeds of the raffle were going to charity, but she knew the publicity would be worth it. She had read Shannon's article in the Sunday paper, and had felt a mixture of pride at the sight of her friend's name, and worry that she wouldn't live up to the expectations set by her grandfather ten years ago.

"What now, Ms. Pacelli?" Iris asked. She was holding an empty container of punch, having just filled up the large bowl next to the pizza buffet.

"I think that's it," Ellie said, looking around. "Just in time, too. Guests have already started arriving."

In no time at all, the pizzeria was filled to the brim. Clara, who had volunteered for the job of leading curious customers around the pizzeria and pointing out the various photographs while telling them about noteworthy points in its history, was already looking frazzled. Jacob was at the door, taking money from the buffet and asking people if they wanted to buy tickets to the raffle, while Rose and Iris — who they had discovered had a gift for cooking - manned the kitchen. Ellie was in the dining area mingling with her guests; a job she usually loved, but today was finding a bit overwhelming. There were just so many people. She was glad when she saw her grandmother's familiar face through the crowd.

"Ellie, it's just wonderful!" the elderly woman said.

"Thanks, Nonna. You helped a lot with those photos." She smiled at her grandmother, then turned her attention to the woman next to her. "Thanks for driving my grandmother over here, Gertie. I know she appreciates it."

"Oh, she does plenty for me. Besides, she promised me one of her famous pies after this, isn't that right, Ann?"

"If you've got any room left after digging into the buffet. I saw how you were eying those pizzas," Nonna said.

Ellie smiled, touched at the sight of the two old woman who had quite obviously known each other for years. She wondered if she would have friends like that when she was her grandmother's age. She had lost touch with most of her friends from Chicago when she moved away, having been too embarrassed to keep up with them after losing both her fiancé and her job in the same day. She might well still be friends with Shannon in forty years, and possibly one or two of the other ladies in their loosely knit group, if she ever had the spare time it would take to get to know them better.

"You two help yourselves. You should take a look at the photos, Nonna. They turned out so well, I think I'll keep them up for good. Clara's giving tours, if you can find her. Oh, and Rose and Iris — she's the new employee, you should go meet her — are going to bring out an Italian wedding themed pizza for the buffet soon. Be sure to save some space for that."

Ellie was eager to try the pizza herself. It had been Rose's idea, based off of Italian wedding soup. It was a thin crust pizza with garlic sauce, small turkey-and-beef meatballs, kale, and spinach covered with Parmesan and asiago cheeses. Her employees had made one to taste test it themselves over the weekend, but she had yet to try a slice.

"Pardon me, but are you Ms. Pacelli?"

Both she and her grandmother looked around. The woman who had spoken was looking at Ellie, so she was the one to respond.

"Yes, I'm Eleanora Pacelli. How may I help, you, Ms....?"

"Martin. Laura Martin," the woman said. She indicated the woman beside her, who could have been her twin. "And this is my sister, Grace."

Martin... the surname sounded familiar, but Ellie couldn't remember where she had heard it. "It's nice to meet you, Ms. Martin. Welcome to Papa Pacelli's. What can I do for you?"

"I was wondering, would you mind taking a picture with my husband and I? For the paper, of course."

"Um, sure. I'd be happy to." She smiled, though she was still at a complete loss as to who the woman actually was.

"Wonderful. My husband should be here soon, then we can get started."

Ellie watched as the woman walked over to the buffet table. Martin... where on Earth had she heard that name?

"That's the mayor's wife," her grandmother whispered, nudging her with her elbow. "You're going to be in the paper with the mayor and his wife. This is going to be wonderful for the restaurant."

Shannon had warned her, or rather, promised her that someone from the newspaper would be there to take pictures, and she would do a follow-up article on the pizzeria's twentieth anniversary. Ellie had dressed accordingly, and was doubly glad that she had worn something nicer than her normal work clothes now that she knew she would be pictured with the mayor.

It wasn't long before Laura Martin found her again, this time accompanied by a man that Ellie recognized instantly — the mayor. He was a distinguished looking man, maybe a decade older than her, in a nice suit and tie. She quickly put down the piece of Italian wedding pizza that she had just bitten into and handed the plate to Clara. Wiping her face with a napkin, she swallowed the bite of pizza as quickly as she dared then cleared her throat and took the man's proffered hand.

"Eleanora Pacelli," she said. "It's so nice to meet you, Mr. Mayor. Welcome to Papa Pacelli's."

"Oh, call me Ambrose. Or Mr. Martin, if you prefer. I was a friend of your grandfather's. Arthur Pacelli was a good man. I'm sorry for your loss."

"Thank you, Mr. Martin. It's been very hard on my grandmother. I didn't know him very well, myself, unfortunately."

"I'll be sure to see Ann before I go and give her my condolences as well. Now, how about that picture for the paper? I'm eager to give that buffet table a spin, but I wouldn't want to be pictured on the front page with pizza sauce on my shirt, would I?"

He chuckled, then waved his hand. A young man with a camera shouldered a couple of people aside. The mayor tugged Ellie and his wife over so they were standing in front of the register, under the hanging banner. He put an arm around his wife, and laid the other hand on the pizzeria manager's shoulder.

"Say cheese," the photographer said dryly. Ellie smiled just as the camera went off with a flash. The photographer checked the screen, then gave them a thumbs up. "All set, Mr. Mayor."

"Thanks, Rufus," the mayor said, dismissing the photographer. "Now, let's go enjoy some of that pizza, my dear."

With that, the Martins made their way back over to the buffet table. Ellie watched them, feeling happy. This party was turning out to be a huge success; she had Shannon to thank for that. If her friend hadn't reminded her of the anniversary, well, then none of this would have happened. This would just be a day like any other.

33

The good mood lasted only a few more minutes. Just as Iris was bringing a second Italian wedding pizza out of the back, a loud groan accompanied by a crashing sound made the entire restaurant go silent. As one, the guests turned to look.

The pizza buffet table had been knocked over, and the mayor's wife was lying next to it, holding her stomach and groaning. The mayor crouched down next to her, looking panicked.

"Someone call an ambulance. Hurry!"

He helped his wife sit up. Ellie could see even from this distance that she was pale. Her hands still clutched at her stomach. She looked around until her eyes landed on the pizzeria manager.

"She did this!" she gasped. "The pizza... it's poisoned!"

CHAPTER FOUR

Ellie groaned and slapped at her nightstand, trying to silence her bleating alarm. When she finally hit the right button and it fell silent, she slitted her eyes open. It was morning. The worst day of her life was officially over, but it was doubtful that this new one would be any better.

"Oh goodness, Bunny. Please tell me that yesterday was a dream."

The little dog wagged her tail, not sure why her owner was upset, but eager to do what she could to cheer her up. It didn't work this time, though.

"Oh my goodness," Ellie repeated, rolling over and pulling the pillow over her eyes as the events from yesterday's disastrous pizza party rushed through her mind. After the mayor's wife had been carted away in an ambulance, there had been no salvaging the event. People hadn't been able to get out of the restaurant fast enough. They hadn't even been able to do the raffle.

"Ellie?" her grandmother called, rapping lightly at the bedroom door. "Are you awake, dear? I brought you tea and toast."

Only the fact that Nonna had made the long climb up the stairway just to bring her food made Ellie get out of bed. "Nonna, you shouldn't have come up here without help," she said, opening the bedroom door. "And definitely not carrying a tray. Here, give me that."

She took the tea tray from her grandmother and placed it on her bed, then took the older woman's arm and helped her towards the stairs.

"I just wanted to help," Nonna said. "I knew you were feeling bad. What happened yesterday wasn't your fault at all."

"I just don't understand what happened," Ellie sighed. "Everyone else was fine after eating the pizzas. I had some, and I'm fine. Do you think she might have been allergic to one of the ingredients?"

"I don't know," her grandmother said, slowly and carefully easing herself down onto the first step. One of her hands gripped the banister, and the other, Ellie's arm. "Maybe it was her appendix." She gave her granddaughter a sly look. "Or maybe she was faking it."

"Why on earth would she fake that?" Ellie asked. "The photographer was still there. She didn't seem like the kind of woman who would want a photo of herself laying on the floor plastered all over the newspapers."

"Oh, that woman always has something up her sleeve to boost her family's publicity. Last election, she had a series of fainting spells, and they always seemed to happen just when Mayor Martin's opponent was in the middle of giving a speech."

"That's horrible of her. She shouldn't fake an illness just for attention. But I don't think that's what it was this time, Nonna. I just don't see how collapsing in the middle of a pizza parlor could benefit her in the slightest."

"You may be right, dear. I'm just saying she recovered mighty quickly, that's all." They had reached the bottom of the stairs, and Ellie let go of her arm.

"You heard something?" she asked.

"It was in the paper this morning," the older woman said.

"Where is it? I want to see."

"Ellie…" Nonna hesitated. "I don't think you do."

"What could be so bad? You said she recovered, right?"

The older woman nodded.

"Then what is it?"

"The paper's in the kitchen," her grandmother said at last, sighing. "Don't say I didn't warn you."

Ellie hurried to the kitchen, where she saw the morning's newspaper open next to her grandmother's half-empty coffee cup. She grabbed and began scanning the pages for the story. It didn't take long; it was on the very front page. *Event at Local Pizzeria Goes Terribly Wrong.* The story went on to detail how the mayor's wife had collapsed during Papa Pacelli's twentieth anniversary party, and had to be taken to the nearest hospital by ambulance. According to the article, she had been discharged just a few hours later, still shaky but mostly recovered. They were calling it food poisoning which, as far as Ellie was concerned, was only slightly better than actual poisoning. The only good thing about the article was that it wasn't written by Shannon.

"I can't believe this," she said, putting down the paper. "This is going to be terrible for the pizzeria."

"Oh, you never know. Some people don't read their papers," her grandmother said, coming into the kitchen.

"Most do. And if people believe this, that the mayor's wife got food poisoning from Papa Pacelli's... well, who's going to want to eat there?"

"This will blow over," the elderly woman said, but she didn't sound as certain as she had before.

"I need to go see Shannon. Maybe she can write something in the next paper, another article retracting this one or something."

Ellie hurried upstairs to get dressed. She downed the tea that her grandmother had brought her, but the toast was mysteriously missing. Bunny was lying next to the tray, looking at her innocently with crumbs in her beard. Despite herself, she laughed.

"You little rascal. You always find a way to make me feel better, don't you? Come on, I'll take you with me to see Shannon if you promise to stop stealing food. Your vet appointment is coming up, and I think you're getting just a tad bit chunky."

Shannon, who must have been one of the first to read the article, told Ellie to come over right away. When she got there, her friend wrapped her in a hug, then invited her and Bunny into the kitchen.

"James left for work already, but he wanted me to tell you that he doesn't think for a heartbeat that Ms. Martin had food poisoning. I was just getting ready to call you. I would have done so earlier, but I didn't want to wake you."

"I just don't understand it, Shannon. Was she really sick, or was she trying to wreck the pizzeria's reputation for some reason?"

"I don't know yet, but I'll do my best to see if I can find out. In the meantime, come on in. We have muffins, or I could defrost you a bagel if you'd like — James buys them in bulk and freezes them, for some reason. I can't stand the things myself."

"A muffin would be great," Ellie said. "I haven't eaten yet. Bunny got my toast."

Within minutes, the two women were sitting in Shannon's kitchen, and Ellie was spreading butter on half of a reheated cinnamon muffin. Bunny was sniffing around the strange kitchen, her tail wagging a mile a minute as she vacuumed up every last crumb from underneath the breakfast table.

"So," Shannon began. "The article. I'm so sorry, Ellie. I refused to write it for them, but that didn't stop them from getting someone else to do it. I told them it wasn't food poisoning. You wouldn't serve bad food."

"This is going to be terrible for the pizzeria." Ellie put down her muffin and rested her head in her hands. "I just can't believe this. Do you think there's any way we could get Ms. Martin to say it wasn't food poisoning? Maybe she has some sort of stomach condition, or... or ate something bad earlier in the day."

"I don't know," her friend said. "She seemed pretty adamant that she got sick from the food at the pizzeria. She gave a statement right after she got out of the hospital."

"Well maybe —"

Shannon's cell phone rang, cutting Ellie off mid-sentence. The journalist gave her an apologetic look, then answered it.

"What is it, Russ?"

That must be Sheriff Ward, Ellie thought. *I wonder if he's read the article yet?*

"Oh my goodness, really?" Shannon paused. "Actually, she's here right now. Yeah, I'll send her over. Thanks for the heads up."

She hung up and put her phone down slowly.

"Ellie, Russell needs to see you at the sheriff's department."

"Okay, but why —"

"Laura Martin's body has just been found. She's dead, Ellie. The mayor's wife is dead."

CHAPTER FIVE

E llie drove to the sheriff's department in a daze. Ms. Martin was dead? *Oh my goodness,* she thought, *if she died from food poisoning, then this will be the end of the pizzeria. What if she really did get some sort of bad food from Papa Pacelli's?* It didn't seem possible, but she hadn't been in the kitchen the whole time. Had one of her employees made a fatal mistake with the food? If so, then why hadn't anyone else gotten sick?

"Eleanora Pacelli here to see Russell Ward," she said to the secretary when she got there. Bunny was on her leash at her side. She had been in too much of a hurry to drop the dog off at home before stopping to see Sheriff Ward.

"I'll let the sheriff know, ma'am," the lady said, giving the little dog a curious look but not commenting on her. "Please take a seat."

In no time at all, Russell made his appearance. He beckoned to her and lead her towards his office, pausing to pat Bunny on her head. She saved her questions until he had shut the door behind them.

"Wha—"

He held up a hand. "Wait, Eleanora. I have to ask you something first." He took a deep breath. "Did you have anything to do with the death of Laura Martin?"

"No! At least… at least, I don't think so."

The sheriff raised an eyebrow. "That's not the usual answer I get from suspects."

"Am I a suspect?" she asked.

He sighed. "Officially, you are a person of interest. I'm sure you understand, after what happened yesterday…"

She nodded. She did understand. The mayor's wife had collapsed in her restaurant, promised never to eat there again, and later that evening had given a statement to a reporter that Papa Pacelli's had given her food poisoning. It was front page news. If anyone had motive to kill Laura Martin, it was Ellie. *I must be at the very top of his list*, she thought.

"And... non-officially? Do you think I did it?"

"I'd like to say no, that I know you well enough to know that you'd never do something like that. But your answer didn't exactly inspire confidence in me." His eyebrow arched higher. "Care to explain exactly how you aren't sure whether or not you killed someone?"

"Well, the food poisoning," Ellie said, looking down at the table in shame. "I'm not saying she got it from Papa Pacelli's, but *if* she did, then it's my fault that she died, isn't it?"

He looked puzzled for a moment, then relieved. She thought she even saw the hint of a smile cross his face. "Ellie, she didn't die from food poisoning. She was strangled."

"Really?" She felt a rush of relief, then guilt at her own reaction. A woman was still dead, after all. "When? Where was she found? Who do you think did it?"

Russell shook his head. "I really can't say any more. It's an ongoing investigation. Well, I suppose I can tell you one thing — she was found at the marina. That, along with the manner of her death, sums

47

up everything the press knows, and I'd like to keep it that way. Now, if you don't mind, I've got some questions I'd like to ask you."

"Of course, go ahead."

"When was the last time you saw Ms. Martin?"

"When she was leaving the pizzeria," she said.

"Did you have any contact with her after that? A phone call or email?"

"No, why? Why would she want to talk to me?"

"I'm afraid I can't say anything else for now. But it's very important that you're honest with me. Are you certain that she didn't get into contact with you? Did anyone give you a message on her behalf?"

"No," Ellie said, shaking her head. "I watched her get loaded into the ambulance, and that was the last I heard of her until I looked at the paper this morning."

"All right, that's good." He made a note. "Where were you between when you left the pizzeria last night and seven o'clock this morning?"

"Home," Ellie said. "I had a late dinner with Nonna, read for a bit, then went to bed. I got up at eight."

"Is there anything else you can think of that might be pertinent to this case?" he asked. "I'm sure you hear a lot, working at the pizzeria."

"Not that I can think of," she told him. "I didn't even know who she was until I saw her husband."

"That's good." He made another note, then leaned back in his seat. "I think that's all for now. Wait, there's actually one more thing." He leaned forward, putting his elbows on the desk and giving her a serious look. "I know you have a habit of getting involved in things you shouldn't. This time, I think it's best for you to stay out of it. Go to work, take care of your grandmother, but stay far away from anything to do with Ms. Martin or her husband. I'm going to tell Shannon the same thing, though I doubt she'll listen to me. Understood?"

"Of course. If she didn't die of food poisoning, then this doesn't have anything to do with me," Ellie said. "Why would I get involved?"

She returned home just in time to take a quick shower before getting ready for work. The house was unusually quiet. Marlowe was hanging on the bars of her cage, watching Ellie closely. The pizzeria manager opened the cage and let the bird step out onto her arm before she made her way towards the kitchen.

"Nonna?" she called. "Are you here?"

No answer. Frowning, she hurried into the kitchen and checked the counter by the phone, where they left each other notes. Sure enough, her grandmother had left her one.

Ellie dear,
I'm going out. Don't worry, I didn't drive myself; Gertie gave me a ride. I'll see you later today!
Love,
Nonna

The note didn't exactly give her very much information, but at least she knew her grandmother was all right. She always dreaded coming home to find that Nonna had fallen and hurt herself.

"I wonder what she's doing?" Ellie said, talking to the bird on her arm. "She doesn't have anything written on the calendar for today." The macaw remained silent, and she shrugged. "Oh, well. I'll ask her about it later. Right now, I've got to get ready to go. The earlier I get to the pizzeria, the better. I want things to be ship-shape for opening. Our reputation can use all of the boost it can get."

CHAPTER SIX

She parked in her usual spot in the back of the pizzeria. No one else was there yet, which wasn't surprising since she had gotten there half an hour before the other employees were scheduled to arrive. There would be plenty of time for her to go through the kitchen without interruption; she was determined to see if she could find any hint of food that had gone bad. Before she went on record saying that the pizzeria had nothing to do with Ms. Martin's food poisoning, she wanted to make sure she had all of the facts.

Ellie pushed open the employee entrance, then froze, realizing her mistake. It hadn't been locked. It should have been locked. She was certain that she had locked up last night; she always locked up. Had one of her employees stopped by for some reason and forgotten to lock the door when they left? No, that wasn't it. The lights were all on, and someone was humming in the dining area. There was somebody there.

Gulping, she eased the employee door shut behind her silently and reached for her phone in her purse. Should she call Russell? What if it was just one of her employees, here early for some reason? Both Iris and Rose lived within walking distance of the pizzeria. Iris didn't have a key yet, though, and Rose wasn't scheduled to work today. Ellie's fingers brushed her phone, but she decided not to make the call yet. The last thing she wanted to do was lead the sheriff on yet another wild goose chase. Besides, what sort of burglar hummed?

Grabbing a spatula as backup, she tiptoed across the floor and pushed the door that lead from the kitchens to the dining are open just an inch. What she saw nearly made her drop the spatula in surprise. Nonna was standing at the register, wiping the counter down with a rag and humming to herself.

"Nonna? What are you doing here?" she asked, coming the rest of the way out of the kitchen.

"I had the most wonderful idea, and I thought I'd surprise you with it," the older woman said, letting the rag fall to the counter and turning to her granddaughter.

"What was your idea?"

"I remembered how you were talking about needing to hire more employees, and since I don't have anything to do most days, I thought why not work here? I helped your grandfather out, you know, when he first opened this place."

"But Nonna, I already hired someone else…" The pizzeria manager fell silent, her eyes on her grandmother's face. She realized that Nonna wasn't doing this to help her out. She was doing this for herself. Ellie thought about just how lonely and quiet the older woman's life must be, without her husband around. If she wanted to spend more time at the restaurant, then her granddaughter wasn't going to stand in her way. "You know what? I think that's a great idea. You know more about this place than any of us. We would love your help here."

Ann Pacelli smiled, her expression grateful. "I don't want to step on your toes, dear. Just think of me the same as any other employee."

"I'll do my best," Ellie said with a chuckle. "I can't promise anything though. You *are* my grandmother, after all."

Clara and Jacob took Nonna's sudden appearance at the restaurant in good stride. It had been years since she had worked there last, so there was a bit of a learning curve as the older woman was taught how to use the modern cash register, but she was a surprisingly quick study. Not that it mattered; she could have taken all day to pick up the new skills and it wouldn't have slowed them down at all. Business at Papa Pacelli's that day was slower than it had ever been before.

"Where is everyone?" Clara asked, a little bit after three. She was sitting in an empty booth, looking around the just as empty dining area. Nonna was perched on the stool behind the register, practicing transactions. Ellie was leaning against the counter, staring out the window, and wishing desperately that just one person would walk through the doors.

"Are you sure the sign's on?" she asked the young woman.

"I triple checked," her employee promised. "It's on."

"At least Jacob has had some deliveries. Maybe people just don't want to show their faces here yet."

At that moment, the kitchen door swung open and Jacob came into the room. He was still wearing his jacket, and his face was flushed.

"I can't believe that," he said, throwing himself into the booth across from Clara. "Three deliveries, and only one of them tipped. The last one didn't even answer the door. I don't know if it was a prank call, or what, but there's a double pepperoni pizza in the kitchen if anyone wants it."

Ellie winced. They didn't get many prank calls; it just wasn't that sort of town. "Add the number to our list, and don't take orders from them anymore. The person who didn't give you a tip... did they say why?"

"No. She just seemed nervous, couldn't get the door shut quickly enough after she took the pizza."

"This is terrible," Ellie groaned, burying her face in her hands. "They think I killed Laura Martin. I just know it."

She looked up when she heard Clara clear her throat. She followed her employee's gaze over to the door, where someone was coming in. Quickly, she straightened up and arranged her expression into a smile. It faded when she saw that it was just Shannon. Her friend would see right through anything false.

"Do you want a pizza?" Ellie asked. "Because if you do, you'd be one of three people in town that do."

"Oh, Ellie, is it really that bad?" Shannon asked, coming over to take her hands. "I had hoped, probably for the first time that I got my job, that no one would read the newspaper."

"I don't know whether people are avoiding this place because of what was printed in the newspaper about Ms. Martin's food poisoning, or because she was found strangled to death just a few hours later," the pizzeria manager said grimly.

"Right now I think it's just the food poisoning," her friend said. "Russell's doing what he can to keep her death quiet for now, though I'm sure a few people will have heard about it through word of mouth. It won't be until the paper comes out tomorrow morning that people will begin avoiding you because they think you killed her."

"Great, so people will be double avoiding me," Ellie sighed.

"I'm going to try to do what I can to help you, but the paper only — oh, hi, Ann." Shannon had just seen Ellie's grandmother, and seemed to be trying to figure out what in the world she was doing standing behind the register with a Papa Pacelli's cap on her head.

"I work here now," Nonna said. She tilted her cap down. "See?"

Shannon nodded. "I sure do. Well, that's nice, isn't it? The two Pacelli women working together."

She turned back to Ellie and raised her eyebrows. The pizzeria manager smiled and shrugged. Her grandmother was healthy and, seemingly, happy; she wasn't one to complain. "What were you saying about the paper?"

"Oh, right," her friend said with a shake. "I was just saying, I'll try to help you and the pizzeria out as much as I can in my column, but the paper only gives me so much freedom. I was thinking of starting a blog or something, but I'd have no idea how to get people to read it. Anyway, I think this will all blow over once Russell finds out who really killed the mayor's wife. It will be much bigger news than her getting sick at the party, and people will forget that soon enough."

"So your advice is to just wait and see?" Ellie asked.

Shannon nodded. "Wait and see, and keep your fingers crossed that another suspect is found as quickly as possible."

CHAPTER SEVEN

Shannon's wait and see strategy only got Ellie so far. Sure enough, the day that Laura Martin's death came out in the newspaper, Papa Pacelli's got even less business than before. She didn't know whether their customers were more scared to be seen in the pizzeria, or more frightened that she was going to leap over the counter and attack them. She began spending most of her hours in the kitchen, happier not to show her face.

Things hardly improved over the next few days. Ellie was glad that she had Thursday scheduled off for Bunny's vet appointment. For all she knew, the restaurant would do better without her there.

Somehow, the papillon seemed to know that they weren't going to one of their usual haunts. She walked slowly behind Ellie on their way to the car, and refused to jump into the seat. Her owner had to pick her up and put her in by force. Ignoring the dog's pitiful look, she walked around to the driver's side door and got in herself.

"You only go to the vet once a year. I don't understand how you can remember the word 'vet' for a whole year, but somehow forget 'sit' after five minutes."

The dog gave one pitiful thump of her tail at the sound of Ellie's voice, then put her head down between her front paws and let out a long sigh. The woman chuckled.

"You sound almost as sad as I've been feeling. I've been kind of self-pitying this week, haven't I?"

The veterinary clinic was down in Benton Harbor, a good twenty minutes' drive from the Pacelli house at the northern edge of town. By the time they reached the highway between the two towns, Bunny had perked up and was looking out the passenger window, her front paws on the car door. Ellie wished that she could find time to enjoy the simple things in life as easily as her dog could, though of course she didn't envy her papillon the poking and prodding she would soon be suffering through at the vet.

"Well, everything looks good," the vet said, giving the little dog a quick scratch behind the ears. "She's set on shots for the next year. Just remember what I said about cutting down on treats. She's only about a pound heavier than I would like, but that's a lot of weight for such a little dog."

"I'll make sure she doesn't get as much between meals," Ellie promised. "She's home a lot during the day with my grandmother, and I've got a suspicion that she gets quite a few extra cookies when I'm not there."

"Increasing her exercise would help, too," the vet said. "But other than her weight, she's perfectly healthy. She seems very well taken care of. Do you have any other pets? We've got a special going right now — fifty percent off an exam for the second pet in your household for new clients."

"Do you see birds?" Ellie asked, thinking of Marlowe. She had no idea when the macaw had last been to see a vet.

"No, sorry. We don't see exotic pets."

"Oh, that's all right. Thanks anyway."

She followed the vet out of the exam room, paid Bunny's bill, and walked outside. Now that the exam was over, the papillon was brimming with energy and jumped right up into the passenger seat when her owner opened the door. Ellie felt better too, surprisingly. The pizzeria was still doing terribly, but it was a nice sunny day, if a bit chilly, and the drive along the coast had done wonders to lift her spirits. It was easy to forget that she lived right by the ocean, and she really spent hardly any time on the water even though her family owned a boat.

Maybe I need to start taking more time to enjoy life, she thought as she guided her car back towards Kittiport. If she had more to her life than work, then maybe she wouldn't get as down when things weren't going so well at Papa Pacelli's. She decided to take advantage of her good mood and stop off at the marina with Bunny before going home. The vet had said that the little dog could use more exercise, and Ellie wasn't exactly in top shape herself.

"Maybe we'll start jogging," she said to her dog. "How would you like that? We'll start slow, but we could both use the exercise."

The marina was busy for the middle of a weekday. Soon enough the weather would be freezing and snowy, so it made sense that people would want to take advantage of this wonderful, clear fall day. Boats were coming and going with such frequency that she was surprised there weren't any crashes. Ellie still wasn't comfortable enough with her grandfather's boat, the *Eleanora* to take it out herself, but she had a book in her purse, and could just as easily kick back on the deck in the marina as she could on the open ocean.

She was halfway down the dock — Bunny in her arms to prevent a repeat of the dog's near-suicidal plunge into the sea — when she remembered that Russell had said that Laura Martin's body had been found here. She didn't know if the woman had been found on a boat, in the water, or on the dock itself. How horrible that must have been for whoever it was that had found her.

Striving to shake off the thoughts of death, Ellie tried to reclaim her good mood. She hopped across to the *Eleanora*, put Bunny down a safe distance from the edge of the boat, and pulled out one of the folding lawn chairs that she used to sun herself on the rare occasions that she and her friends took the boat out.

She managed to lose herself in her book for a few minutes, but the docks were too busy for any real peace. The brisk sea breeze was chillier than she had thought, and the occasional scent of fish wafted over to her. Putting the book down, she leaned back and closed her eyes, determined to at least enjoy the sun for a few minutes before heading back home and facing life again.

"Eleanora?"

She jolted upright. "Russell?" The sheriff was standing on the dock, watching her.

"Sorry for disturbing you. I was just surprised to see you somewhere other than at the pizzeria," he said. He was in his uniform, which meant that he was on the job.

"I do have a life outside of work," she said. "Sort of. Bunny had a vet appointment today, and it was so nice out that I decided to stop here on my way back from Benton Harbor."

"I don't blame you. If it wasn't for the murder, I would probably have taken today off and gone fishing. Is everything all right with Bunny?" He peered down at the little dog, who was passed out in the sunlight.

"She's a bit overweight, but other than that she's as healthy as a horse," Ellie said. "It was just her annual checkup."

"Ah. That's good. She's been through quite a lot lately."

She wondered if he was thinking of the little dog's fall off the dock, or that time she had gotten lost in the woods, or both. Probably both, she decided.

"She's a tough little pup," she said. "So, what are you doing here? Looking into Ms. Martin's death, still?"

"Yes, though I haven't been able to find much." He stepped to the edge of the dock to let a group of people pass, then nodded at the *Eleanora* and raised his eyebrows. "Can I come aboard?"

"Of course, make yourself at home," she said. He stepped off the dock onto the boat, then crouched next to Bunny and began petting her. The little dog didn't seem to mind being woken up from her nap in the slightest.

"To be honest," he said in a lower voice, "I haven't had much luck making any progress on this case at all. I came here to look around in the off chance that some evidence was overlooked before. I've been asking some of the boat owners if they'd seen or heard anything, but haven't had any luck yet with that either."

"You're looking around for evidence?" Ellie asked. "Here? Was she near my grandfather's boat?"

He shook his head. "She was discovered a bit closer to the parking lot, nearer shore. I've been walking all over the marina in the off chance the current carried something this way."

"I'm sorry. I know how much it must bother you, not having any leads on who the killer is."

"Well, at least we've managed to eliminate a few people from our pool of suspects." He brightened. "Actually, you aren't a person of interest in the case anymore, Ellie. Forensics put her death at around six o'clock Monday night. I called the pizzeria just to be sure, and your employees verified that you were there until at least eight."

"That's good. Great, in fact," Ellie said brightly. "Do you think the paper will say anything about that? We might get more customers at the pizzeria if people don't think I'm a murderess."

"I've already told Shannon," he said, smiling. "I'm sure she'll figure out a way to work your innocence in somehow." He stood up and brushed off his knees. "Thanks for the talk. I should get back to work. There must be *something* I'm missing."

He stepped off the boat, hesitated, then turned back to her. "Actually, there's one more thing."

69

"Go ahead," Ellie said as she gathered up her things, preparing to leave herself.

"Would you like to go out to dinner with me sometime?"

Her book slipped from her fingers. She quickly grabbed it and shoved it in her purse, using the extra few seconds to think. Was he asking her out? On a real date? Or was he just asking her as a friend? She didn't have the courage to ask, but it didn't matter because her answer would be the same either way.

"Sure," she said. "That sounds nice."

CHAPTER EIGHT

llie practically skipped into work the next morning. As much as she told herself not to get her hopes up about her dinner with the sheriff — she was best friends with his sister-in-law, after all, he probably just wanted to get to know her better — her heart beat a little faster whenever she thought about it. He wasn't exactly the sort of man she usually dated, but maybe that was a good thing. He was a good man, a down to earth man, and she already felt like she could count on him.

She'd told Shannon about their dinner the second she got home, and her friend hadn't seemed to know what to think either.

"He doesn't usually date," she had said. "In fact, I think he's only gone on one date since his wife died, and that was something James set up. It, erm, didn't go well."

"Even if he just wants to get to know me better as friends, that's okay," Ellie said. "No offense to you, but I need more than one good friend in this town."

"None taken," her friend had replied with a chuckle. "Call me afterward, and we can talk."

Things were looking up in other ways, too. Papa Pacelli's got a couple of customers within a few hours of opening, maybe not as many as they usually got, but definitely a lot better than they'd been doing for the past few days. *It's too soon for anything to be in the paper about my alibi,* she thought. *People must just be beginning to forget. Or they're deciding that a good slice of pizza is worth the chance of running into the crazy Pacelli woman.*

She managed to get halfway through the day before things began going downhill. It all started when she was at the register, ringing a customer up, and Iris came out of the kitchen to hand over the man's pizza.

"Who's that?" she said as he walked away. Ellie followed her gaze. There were two people standing out in front of the pizzeria, carrying what looked like big signs, the sort that she had seen people carry to protests.

"I have no idea," she said. "Is something going on in town today? Some sort of rally, maybe?"

The young woman shrugged, then shook her head. "No, not that I know of."

"Hmm. Watch the register for me. I'll be right back in."

Ellie walked towards the door, a suspicion beginning to sneak up on her. She was certain that she would have recognized that curly hair anywhere.

"Xavier," she said coldly as she stepped outside. "And Jeffrey? What are the two of you up to?"

Xavier had worked at the pizzeria for two years before she took over. She had fired him the instant that she discovered his long history of stealing money from the restaurant. He had been hired shortly thereafter by the man who owned Cheesaroni Calzones; Jeffrey Dunham. Cheesaroni was Papa Pacelli's main competition in Kittiport. Ellie had only eaten there once; the food was good, but the service left a lot to be desired.

"Exercising our rights of free speech," Xavier said, spinning the sign around so she could read it. *Don't support Murder. Don't eat at Papa Pacelli's.* Jeffrey did the same. His sign read, *If you want good food without a trip to the hospital, eat at Cheesaroni Calzones.*

"You can't... what do you think... how dare you..." the pizzeria manager spluttered. "This isn't free speech! This is slander. It's illegal. Get out of here right now before I call the cops."

"Last time I checked, poisoning someone and then killing them wasn't legal either," Jeffrey said. "So go ahead and call whoever you like. I'm sure the media would just love it if we emailed them some pictures of the police going into your restaurant."

Ellie glared at them, but she had the feeling that she was caught. If they took pictures of the police pulling up to the pizzeria, they could spread the photos around with whatever explanation they liked. The last thing that she wanted was for the public to think that there was some sort of investigation underway at Papa Pacelli's. Besides, she didn't actually know if what they were doing was illegal or not. Did she really have any other option than to just ignore them and hope that no one believed their ridiculous claims?

"You guys are sad, you know?" she said as she turned to go back inside. "You have to put down someone else's business just to get

75

customers at your own place. At least I can say that I've never had to lie to get customers."

She let the door swing shut behind her on their snickering and walked back over to the register, where Iris was waiting. "Ignore them," she said. "Hopefully no one will pay any attention to them."

Unfortunately, potential customers seemed to take the warnings on the signs to heart, either that or they just didn't feel like walking past the two sign-carrying men to get inside the restaurant. Besides a few delivery orders, they hardly had any customers for the next few hours.

"What should we do?" Iris asked gazing anxiously out the window. Jacob, who had just gotten back from the last round of deliveries, frowned. Ellie listened, but didn't join in on the conversation. She was too busy glaring at the back of Xavier's head. The young man had been a thorn in her side since she'd moved back to Kittiport.

"We need to get back at them somehow," Jacob said. "Give them a taste of their own medicine."

"But how? They haven't been accused of anything bad."

"That's not quite true," Ellie said, breaking her silence at last. She glanced over to Jacob, who looked puzzled for a moment, then grinned.

"Oh, yeah. You're right," he said. "Did you ever go to the police about his stealing?"

"No. At the time, I had too much else on my hands, trying to get this place up and running again. But I still have all of the old records. I could go to the sheriff with the proof."

"You do that," Jacob said. His grin widened. "I have an idea of my own of how to get back at them."

Ellie raised an eyebrow. "It's nothing illegal, is it?"

"Oh, no. I think you'll like this…" He explained his idea to her, and her face broke into a wide smile. It was the perfect plan. She didn't know why she hadn't thought of it sooner.

CHAPTER NINE

"What do you think, Bunny? It's been a while since I've worn this dress. I haven't gained too much weight?"

She took the dog's silence to mean no, she hadn't. The dark green dress — which coincidentally matched her car nearly to the shade — *did* look pretty good on her, even if it showed off her curves a bit more than she would have liked. She had dithered between a dress and a pantsuit for a long time, but she thought that her pantsuits made her look too severe; perfect for the high intensity financial world that she had left behind, but not what she wanted for her dinner with Russell.

She had ended up deciding on one of her more casual dresses. She still wasn't sure if the sheriff considered their dinner a date, or just a meal between friends. What she *did* know was that they had definitely been on much more casual terms since he had helped her solve one of her family's mysteries. She didn't know exactly what she had done to earn his trust, since the whole thing had ended in disaster, but she was glad to have the beginnings of a friendship with him.

Craning her head in an attempt to look at her back, still a bit sensitive about the weight that she had gained in the past few months — managing a pizza place and getting as many free pizzas as she wanted, *good* free pizzas, wouldn't have been good for anyone's form — Ellie decided to call it good enough. She could spend hours digging through her closet, and she probably wouldn't find anything that fit her perfectly. It was time to focus on her hair and make-up, or else she would risk being late to the White Pine Kitchen.

Ellie recognized the sheriff's truck in the restaurant's parking lot and smiled to herself. He had offered to pick her up, but she always felt more comfortable driving herself, an old habit left over from before she met her ex-fiancé, when she used to go out on dates with people she hardly knew. The last thing she had wanted was to be dependent on a near stranger for a ride home, especially if the date hadn't gone well. Of course, Russell was far from being a stranger, but old habits die hard, and she had reflexively told him that she would meet him there.

He was waiting just inside the doors for her, and smiled when he saw her. She had only ever seen him in nice clothes once before; the night of their fake dinner date when her family had been visiting. He was usually dressed in either his sheriff's uniform, or fishing gear, so it was a nice change.

"You look nice," he said. "Our table should be ready in just a minute."

He had barely gotten the words out of his mouth when the hostess called out a table for two, under the name Ward. Ellie followed the woman into the restaurant to a booth by one of the windows.

"A server will be by in just a moment to take your drink orders," the hostess said brightly before walking off.

Left alone with Russell at the table, Ellie felt suddenly self-conscious. What did they even have to talk about? Would the whole meal be filled with awkward silences? Why had she thought this was a good idea? Desperate for something to say, she latched onto the topic that had been at the forefront of her mind all week.

"Any luck with the case?"

Russell seemed to relax a little bit at the familiar subject. "Unfortunately, no. It seems like no one saw anything, even though I must have spoken with half of the people who use the marina by now. There are a few video cameras in lots adjacent to the marina, but none of them were filming the right spot at the right time to be useful. I found a clip of Ms. Martin's car driving towards the parking lot by the docks, but it's too dark to see inside the vehicle, so there's no way to tell if she was alone in the vehicle — or if she was even driving it herself. For all I know, she could have been killed elsewhere, then dumped at the marina."

"It must be frustrating," Ellie said empathetically. "It's a pretty high profile case, isn't it? Has the mayor been pushing you for progress? I imagine that he's absolutely devastated."

"He's been patient," Russell said. A frown creased his brow for a moment, but his expression quickly cleared.

"Do you think he could have done it?" she asked, keeping her voice quiet. "I mean, if someone I loved had been killed, I'd be beating down your door trying to get answers."

"I don't doubt that," he said with a chuckle. "I really can't talk about any specifics of the case until it's solved. I'm sorry."

"It's okay, I understand," she said, sighing. "I know you told Shannon and I not to get involved, but I can't help it. I want to see this case solved as much as you do. Besides simple curiosity, it's still affecting my restaurant."

At that moment their waiter showed up. The conversation halted while they gave their drink orders, and Ellie realized that she hadn't even glanced at the menu yet. She had no idea what she would order when the waiter came back. Everything looked delicious, though she knew the one thing that she did not want was the lobster pizza. It didn't seem right, to work at a pizzeria and then order pizza at another restaurant when she went out to dinner.

"What do you mean, it's still affecting the pizzeria?" Russell asked suddenly, putting down his menu and looking at her with a concerned expression.

"Well —" she began, but the waiter had come back with their drinks, and was ready to take their order.

"The chicken cordon bleu, please," Russell said distractedly.

"And you, ma'am?"

"Um, the lemon pecan brook trout, please. With the roasted redskins. Thanks," Ellie said.

"Hey, aren't you the lady that owns that pizzeria?" the waiter asked as he took the menu from her. The couple at the next table fell silent and turned in their seats to look.

"I don't own it, my grandmother does," she told him. "But yes, I manage Papa Pacelli's."

"Neat. Is it true that you killed some woman who didn't like your pizza?"

Ellie gaped at him. "No, that is most definitely *not* true," she said. "Where in the world did you hear that?"

"My girlfriend's mom told her not to eat there anymore because you killed someone," the young waiter said. He suddenly seemed to realize that he had just accused a guest of murder, and quickly backpedaled. "But, I mean, I don't believe it. I love your pizza. It's a great restaurant. Uh, your fish will be right out." He hurried away. The couple at the next table began whispering to each other.

"That's what I mean," she told Russell quietly. "Rumors. People think I'm responsible for Ms. Martin's death."

As if to prove her point, the couple at the next table flagged down the waiter, and a moment later, hurried away, their food left uneaten. Russell stared after them, his gaze cold.

"There's absolutely no reason you should be linked to her death," he said turning back to her. "You were never even an official suspect."

"All they know," she said, meaning the general populace of Kittiport, "is that the woman was driven away from my pizzeria in an ambulance, and was found dead later that night. The details don't matter to them. It doesn't help that Xavier and Jeffrey have been hanging around in front of the pizzeria, waving signs that warn people that I'm a killer."

"I'll see what I can do about that," he told her. "I'm sorry, Ellie. The last thing I wanted was for you to get dragged into this."

"It's not your fault," she said. "It's just, well, bad luck. Once the real murderer is caught, things should go back to normal… I hope."

Despite her words, Ellie didn't have much hope. She picked at her food when it came, hardly noticing the mouthwatering flavors of the pecan-encrusted fish. The reaction of the couple, who had gotten up and left when they found out who she was, hurt far more than Xavier and Jeffrey picketing. She expected that much from them, but to think that she had become such a pariah to people who didn't even know her struck her to the bone.

CHAPTER TEN

B ringing up the case during dinner had been a mistake. She should have started talking about something else — anything else. For the rest of the meal, they mulled over ideas for how to boost the pizzeria's reputation, but Ellie knew that both of their minds were on the real puzzle; who had killed Laura Martin?

After they were finished with dessert, the sheriff walked her to her car, and they stood there for a moment in the chilly night air. "I had a nice time," Ellie said at last.

"Me too," he said. "Thanks for coming. I'm sorry our conversation wasn't over a cheerier topic."

"Well, at least I got to pick your brain for ideas. I'm glad you like the plan that Jacob came up with."

"I think Papa Pacelli's should have done it a long time ago," he said. "Who doesn't love a good calzone?"

"I'll expect you to be first in line," she told him with a smile.

She was tired by the time she got back home, and it felt amazingly good to curl up under her blankets with Bunny on the pillow next to her head, comfortably warm in her room while a cold wind blew outside. Her thoughts oscillated between the subject of the murder, and dinner. She was in an odd mood, and more than anything wanted to talk to someone about her night, but Shannon wasn't likely to appreciate a call this late at night. Bunny, though a great listener, was a terrible conversationalist. Anything Ellie wanted to discuss, would just have to wait until morning.

The next day started off well, with fresh blueberry muffins and a quick jog with Bunny. Well, it was mostly a walk, with a couple of faster steps thrown in for good measure. Still, everyone had to start somewhere, and neither of them were in the best of shape. Half a mile to Ellie might as well have been three miles to the papillon.

When she got to work, she was happy to see that Jeffrey and Xavier weren't in front of the pizzeria with their signs. Whether they weren't coming at all, or simply weren't there yet, she didn't know. She hoped the former, but either way, she and Jacob were going to spend a few hours working on his plan this afternoon.

Having skipped the early lunch that her grandmother had offered, Ellie was starved. The whole point of skipping the meal had been to make up for some of the calories that she had eaten the night before, all in line with her new goal of getting both herself and Bunny back in shape. Unfortunately, the promise of a custom, fresh-made personal pizza with all of her favorite toppings and extra cheese was just too much for her to resist. Once the ovens were fired up, she quickly rolled out a small ball of dough and let it pre-cook while she continued preparing to open the restaurant. By the time Rose and Jacob arrived, she was sitting at the kitchen table, halfway done with her bacon, chicken, and pineapple personal pizza with extra cheese. *Note to self*, she thought, *don't skip lunch. Being hungry destroys what little self-control I have.*

Maybe thanks to the fact that Xavier and Jeffrey seemed to have given up on their little sign-waving venture, the pizzeria was busier that day than normal. Well, the new normal; it was still well below how it had been before the whole fiasco with the mayor's wife. Ellie was relieved that they actually had customers again, though she couldn't help but wonder exactly how long it would take before they were back up to pre-disaster standards.

Once again deciding that she would best serve the pizzeria by hiding in the back, so as not to frighten away the cautious customers, Ellie let Rose spend her entire shift at the register. Since that was usually a more coveted position than working in the kitchen, where it was stifling hot at the best of times, she was surprised to see her employee come into the back and tie an apron around her waist.

"There's someone here to see you," Rose said. "I'll take over back here if you want."

"Who is it?" Ellie asked, putting down the spoon that she had been using to ladle sauce and going over to the sink to wash up.

"She said her name was Grace Camper," Rose said. "Which order is this?"

"Number twenty-three, thin crust with green peppers and ham," the pizzeria manager answered automatically. Then, as her brain caught up with her mouth, she added, "Grace Camper? I've never heard of her. Did she say what she wanted?"

"She said she wanted to talk to you, but that's it," her employee said. She gave her boss a concerned look. "Is everything all right?"

Ellie shook her head. "I don't know. To be honest, with everything that's been happening, I doubt she wants anything good."

She pushed through the kitchen doors, then stopped in her tracks. The woman in front of her was familiar; she had a face that Ellie would never forget. How could she, after having been accused of murdering the woman?

"Laura Martin?" she squeaked. She realized her face immediately, as the other woman's face crumpled.

"No, I'm her sister," she said. "Grace."

"I'm so sorry," Ellie said, her cheeks flaming with embarrassment. "I know I met you at the party. You just look so much like her…"

"I know. I'm two years older than her, but we look like we're twins." The woman's breath caught. "Or I guess I should say 'looked' and 'were.'"

"I can't even imagine what you're going through right now," the pizzeria manager said. "Is there anything I can get you? Rose said you wanted to talk to me. What can I do to help?"

"Can you sit?" Grace asked, indicating a table with a nod of her head. "I want to ask for your help with something, but it might take a little bit of explaining."

"Of course."

They sat, and Ellie waited quietly for the woman to gather her thoughts. At last, she took a deep breath and said, "I think Laura was killed by her husband."

"The mayor?"

Grace nodded grimly.

"Have you gone to the police? Why do you think that he killed her?"

"I don't want to go to the police until I have some sort of proof," she said, a look of fear flashing through her eyes. "If they question him, but don't have enough to hold him, then who's to say he won't come after me next?"

"I'm sure Russ— the sheriff would protect you," Ellie said. "What makes you think the mayor did it?"

"I think one of them was having an affair," the other woman said, lowering her voice even though there was no one else in the restaurant. "She was alone with him that evening. He said that she decided to go out on a walk alone, but there's no alibi, no one can say for sure whether she went alone, or if he followed her."

The pizzeria manager was nodding. Especially after what Russell said about the mayor, it seemed plausible. "Why come to me, though?"

"Because I heard that you were friends with one of the women that writes for the paper. I thought maybe you could ask her to do some digging on both my sister and her husband. If she can find some sort of proof that one of them was having an affair, then that might be enough proof to put the mayor away, or at least make the police take us seriously. I know you probably want the whole thing over and done with as much as I do."

A glance around the conspicuously empty restaurant drove the point home. "I'll do what I can to help," Ellie said. "You keep trying to find some sort of proof, too. Between the two of us, and Shannon, we should be able to come up with something good."

CHAPTER ELEVEN

P romising Grace that she would help find the person who killed her sister was one thing. Actually doing it was another. Ellie was immediately tempted to go to Russell with what she knew, but realized that the woman's concerns were legitimate. If the mayor really had murdered his wife, then what were the chances that he would feel bad about doing her sister in, too? If Russell questioned him, and he got the feeling that Grace had something to do with it, then her life very well could be in danger.

She ended up doing just what the woman had suggested; she went to Shannon the next morning. Her friend was more than happy to meet her at a cafe in town, eager to hear more details about her date with Russell. They had only been able to cover so much over the phone, and before Ellie got down to the real reason for their meeting, she went over the night of the dinner once more.

"I can't believe they just got up and left," her friend said, fixated on the couple that had abandoned their meal after realizing just who it was they had been seated next to.

"It was pretty terrible," Ellie agreed. "I can't believe how quickly word spread around town. Well, word about the bad stuff. The fact that I'm actually innocent doesn't seem to be making any headway at all."

"Oh, it can't be that bad. You said yourself that you've been getting more customers lately."

"We still aren't nearly as busy as we were before all of this," she pointed out. "But anyway, that's not why I wanted to meet you. I know I messed up dinner with your brother-in-law pretty badly; I don't want to relive it over coffee."

"Sorry," Shannon said. "I don't think you messed anything up, though. Russ is a good guy. He'll understand that you're going through a hard time right now. Since you brought it up, what exactly was the reason you wanted to meet? You wouldn't say very much on the phone."

Ellie took a sip of her slightly-too-sweet coffee, then leaned forward and in a hushed voice, told her friend what Grace had told her.

"So she wants our help in tracking down an affair we don't even know for sure exists?" Shannon said when she was done, one eyebrow arched.

"She seemed to be pretty certain about it."

"Did she gave you any names?"

Ellie hesitated, then shook her head. "No names."

"Do you really think the mayor did it?" her friend asked.

"Maybe. Russell did say that he didn't seem too upset about the whole thing."

Shannon sighed. "Well, I'll do some digging, but I'm not promising you anything, okay? It would help if I had names, dates, anything to go on, really."

"Grace said she's going to look for proof too. So between the three of us, we should be able to find something."

"If there's anything to find," her friend said. "I wouldn't hold my breath."

Ellie left their coffee date in time to make it to the pizzeria for opening. Today was a big day, and she didn't want to miss it. Besides, Nonna was planning on working there again for a few hours, and she had to make sure her grandmother got settled in okay and remembered how to use the register correctly.

Jacob was already getting started on their big surprise, and Ellie shared a mischievous grin with him as she passed through the kitchen. She couldn't wait to see the reaction of the crew at Cheesaroni when they found out what their competitors were planning. And, even better, her crew at Papa Pacelli's didn't have to drag anyone's name through the mud to get their revenge.

"Hey, Nonna," she said as she walked into the dining area. "Are you sure you're up to this today?"

"Yes I am," her grandmother replied. "I'm old, that doesn't mean I'm made out of glass, you know. I could do more than sit behind this register all day, if your employees didn't all act like I could break at any moment."

"They're just concerned about you," she said. "Besides, the customers love seeing you out front at the register. You're the face of Papa Pacelli's."

"Oh, that was your grandfather, and I make a poor fill-in for him," the older woman said. "But I suppose you're right. There should be a Pacelli out front to greet the customers. It's a job I'll proudly do."

Ellie smiled to herself as she walked across the room to unlock the front door. She enjoyed having her grandmother there. She would never admit it to the older woman, but she was almost like their mascot, and she suspected that her employees felt the same way. Even the customers seemed to like Nonna best; they always left the most in the tip jar when she was the one at the counter.

She had just unlocked the door when a familiar form walked into view. It was Russell, walking along the sidewalk towards the pizzeria. He waved when he saw her watching him.

"Hey," he said as she opened the door for him. "I just thought I'd stop by and see how everything is going. Any more trouble from those guys at the calzone place?"

She shook her head. "Thankfully, no. They must have gotten bored, standing out there all day. Can you stay for about half an hour? Jacob's putting the first batch of our revenge plan into the oven as we speak."

"Sure. I'll be the first in line to buy one," he said, grinning. He glanced at the register, then did a double-take. "Is that your grandmother?"

Ellie looked over her shoulder. Nonna gave a wave. "Yep, that's her. She works here part time now. Her decision. I think it's been too quiet around the house for her taste."

Smiling, Sheriff Ward walked over to the counter to say hello, while Ellie grabbed a poster out of the supply cupboard and prepared to hang it on the window. It was almost time for the grand reveal.

CHAPTER TWELVE

"What do you think?" Ellie asked anxiously, watching the sheriff's face as he chewed.

"This is seriously the best calzone I've had, Ellie," he said when he swallowed. "I think you've found your new calling."

Ellie smiled with relief, then turned her attention to the half calzone on her own plate. She cut a bite off and dipped it in the cup of pizza sauce next to her plate before popping it in her mouth. It *was* good; their first full batch of calzones had turned out even better than the practice one they had made the other day. Gooey cheese, pepperoni, mushrooms, and fresh basil leaves along with the famous Papa Pacelli's crust combined to make a heavenly pocket of goodness.

"This is perfect," she agreed. "I can't believe I didn't think of this before. It has got to be *the* best way of getting back and Xavier and

Jeffrey for everything they've done over the past few months. They seem determined to run this restaurant into the ground, so I don't feel bad at all giving them some real competition."

"I bet this will boost your sales, even with everything else that's going on," Russell said, glancing at the new poster in the window, which read *Now serving calzones!* in big letters, with a picture of their practice calzone underneath, Somehow, Jacob had even managed to capture the steam in the photo as it rose from the cut-open dough. It was a mouth-watering advertisement, sure to draw in hungry guests.

"I sure hope so," Ellie said. "I just need to get the word out. We probably won't get too many people passing by on foot in this weather."

It had started to rain since Russell got there, a cold drizzle that showed no sign of letting up. It wasn't a great day for advertising their new calzones, but at least she was certain that the duo from Cheesaroni wouldn't show up.

"I'll go tell the guys and gals at the sheriff's department," he said, getting up. "We usually order lunch on Fridays anyway. I'll see if they want to try your calzones."

"Half off orders to the sheriff's department," Ellie said. "I don't see how anyone could turn down that offer."

"Me either. Thanks for the food, and I'm glad those guys aren't bothering you anymore. I'm sure you'll be getting a call from the department soon about those calzones." He nodded to her, then zipped his jacket and flipped his hood up, pausing to eye the cloudy sky before stepping out into the wet day.

Just as he was leaving, someone else came in. She gave the sheriff a wide berth, shooting an anxious glance from him to Ellie as she let the door close between them.

"Don't worry, Grace," the pizzeria manager said. "I didn't mention anything about what you told me."

"Thanks," the woman said, looking relieved. "I'm just so scared he's going to know I'm onto him. Did you get a chance to talk to your friend at the paper?"

"I did. She is happy to help, but we really need more to go on. Why do you think one of them was having an affair?"

"They've both acting weird for the past couple of weeks. Laura would cancel lunch together just minutes before she was supposed to be there, or just not show up at all. My brother-in-law started wearing a new cologne, and I swear I heard him tell his assistant that he couldn't make a meeting because he had a date once. Just little things like that. Maybe they were both having affairs, or maybe Laura knew that he was up to something and was trying to follow him. That's my guess, though I have no idea why she wouldn't have told me if that's the case. Anyway, I came here to give you these."

She reached into her purse and pulled out an envelope, which she put on the table. Ellie reached for it and glanced inside. Photos.

"It's from the security camera outside of their house. I convinced the housekeeper to let me see the footage. If you can find out who that woman is, then maybe one of us can go and talk to her. She might know something."

Ellie began looking through the pictures. They were all of the same woman, an attractive brunette, at the Martin's front door. The photos were dated and had time stamps.

"Wow, she's been going over there for months," she said. "You think this is who the mayor was having an affair with? You don't have any idea who she is?"

"No, I don't. I thought your journalist friend might be able to help you with that."

"Do you really think he would have killed his wife if she confronted him about this?" Ellie asked.

"That... or maybe he got tired of leading a double life," the other woman whispered. "I think that this was premeditated."

"Why?"

"Well, we both know that my sister didn't get food poisoning from the pizzeria."

**

Grace left Ellie with a stack of photos, and a lot to think about. She desperately wanted to go to Russell with everything, but loathed to be the woman who cried wolf. She had been wrong about this sort of thing before. She decided that Grace was right. They needed more proof, some sort of solid evidence of an affair, before going to him.

ITALIAN WEDDING MURDER:BOOK FOUR IN PAPA PACELLI'S PIZZERIA SERIES

These photos were a good start, but for all she knew the woman was a housekeeper or a real estate agent, or had any number of legitimate reasons for being there.

She wanted to call Shannon and start looking for the mystery woman right away, but things were starting to pick up in the pizzeria. School had gotten out for the day, and a few bedraggled teens had made their way to the restaurant, and Ellie smelled her very first calzone sale approaching. There would be time to solve murders later.

CHAPTER THIRTEEN

T he calzones were a huge success. Ellie made a mental note to give Jacob a raise when this was all over; it had been his brilliant idea. Even some of the people who had been avoiding them like the plague since the disastrous party had stopped in to try the new dish, and she had already gotten several requests and ideas for different flavors of calzone.

The pizzeria was busy right up to closing time, and they were all exhausted by the time they could finally lock up and go home. Nonna had ended up staying all day to help out, something that Ellie wasn't too happy about. Those were long hours for a woman in her eighties to be working. The pizzeria manager had just enough time to stop by Shannon's and drop the photos off before driving home and helping her exhausted grandmother into bed.

The next morning was a quiet one in the Pacelli house. It was a Saturday, so Ellie had no plans to go in to the pizzeria, though she would call later in the day and see how things were going. The success of the calzones had lifted a weight of anxiety off of her chest. The pizzeria wasn't going to go under; despite everything, they were going to pull through.

Deciding to take full advantage of her day off, Ellie settled down in the living room with a plate of maple fudge no-bake cookies and the television controls. She flipped through the channels until she found a show that she recognized, then pulled a blanket over her lap and settled in for a long day of nothing but relaxing. Bunny was curled up on the cushion next to her, and Marlowe was perched on the back of the easy chair in the corner, her head tucked under her wing. Nonna was taking a nap in her room, still worn out from her long day the day before.

It wasn't long before Ellie dozed off herself. When her phone rang, she woke up with a jolt. The plate of cookies fell off her lap and onto the floor. Rather, the plate fell to the floor. The cookies themselves were nowhere to be found, though the crumbs on the couch cushion next to the papillon told the story of what had happened clearly enough.

"I can't believe you took those right off the plate, your sneaky little dog," Ellie grumbled as she fumbled for her cell phone. The number was the pizzeria's. "Hello?"

"Ms. Pacelli, you have to come and see this, right now!"

It was Clara. She sounded panicked.

"What is it?" Ellie asked, sitting bolt upright. "Are you okay?"

"I'm not hurt, it's the pizzeria... oh, you have to see it for yourself. Please, hurry. I'm going to call the police."

She was up in a flash, quickly putting the macaw back in her cage and pulling on her jacket over her old t-shirt. She shoved her feet into a pair of boots, and hurried out the door. Scenarios kept playing through her mind, getting steadily worse as she wove through the scant traffic on her way into town.

She pulled into a spot on the street in front of Papa Pacelli's and leapt out of the car. She didn't have to look for long to find out what had caused the panicked call minutes before. There was something red splattered across the front windows of the pizzeria, and spray painted in big, black letters across the door was the word *murderer*.

"Oh my goodness," she breathed, putting a hand out to lean on her car for support. The spray paint was bad enough, but what was that red stuff? Blood?

"Pizza sauce," a voice from behind her said, making her jump.

She spun around and saw Russell. His truck was parked right behind her car. She must not have seen it in her hurry to reach the pizzeria.

"Are you sure?" she asked. He nodded.

"Bethany and I got here a couple of minutes ago. She's inside taking a statement from Clara right now. If you get closer, you can smell it. It's definitely pizza sauce. I know it must be hard to see your place like this, but I promise we're going to do everything that we can to find out who did it."

"I know who did it," Ellie said, her voice shaking with rage. "Jeffrey and Xavier." Who else would have splashed gallons of pizza sauce on the front of her restaurant?

"We'll question them as soon as we're done here," he promised. "Listen, I know you might want to do something to get even with them, but it isn't worth it. Things will just keep escalating until someone gets hurt. They committed a crime, and it's in the hands of the law now. Understand?"

Gritting her teeth, she nodded. "Do you think they did this because we started selling calzones?"

"If I had to guess, yeah. I'd say that's what drove them over the edge."

He sighed and ran his hands through his hair. "I'm really sorry about this, Ellie. I can help you clean up —"

"No," she said. "Thanks, but we can handle it. I don't want to keep you from questioning the two guys over at Cheesaroni. The sooner you get a confession from them, the better."

"All right," he said. "I'll stop by later and see how things are going. In the meantime, maybe start doing some research on security systems. If you had them on camera doing this, charging them would be a lot easier."

Ellie was shaking with anger the entire time that she and Clara were cleaning off the building. She had no regrets about selling calzones and competing directly with Cheesaroni. If anything, she was more

ITALIC

certain than ever that she had made the right choice. She had the feeling that this was the beginning of a long war between the two restaurants, but she was confident that Papa Pacelli's could come out ahead. Once this whole murder and food poisoning scandal blew over, she was certain that the addition of calzones to her menu would make the pizzeria more popular than ever. Cheesaroni Calzones wouldn't stand a chance unless they stopped focusing so much on her restaurant, and started focusing more on their own.

The pizza sauce was easy enough to hose off, but the spray paint was a different story. They ended up having to scrape it off the glass, and it took hours. When the front of the pizzeria at long last looked normal again, Ellie breathed a sigh of relief. Realizing that she had left in such a hurry that she had forgotten to leave a note for her grandmother, she returned to her car and fished her cell phone out of her purse. She was surprised to see three missed calls, all from Shannon.

"What is it?" she asked when she called her friend back.

"I spent the morning searching online," Shannon said, her voice tinged with excitement. "And I found her, Ellie. I found the woman in the photos."

CHAPTER FOURTEEN

After making sure that Clara and Rose were comfortable keeping an eye on the pizzeria alone after what had happened, Ellie got back into her car and drove to Shannon's house. James answered her knock and welcomed her in.

"Shannon's in her office," he said. "I have no idea what you two are doing, but she practically burst my eardrums with her squeal of excitement earlier this morning. She must be on to something good."

Ellie hurried through the house and knocked on the closed door to the room that her friend used as a home office. Shannon answered immediately, telling her to come on in.

"You found her?"

"I did. It didn't even take that long," her friend said.

"How? Who is she?"

"Well, I figured that regardless of whether or not she's having an affair with the mayor, he must know her somehow. So I began looking through old newspapers, looking for photos of her with him. I found this one of him at the last election. Look, she's in the background."

Ellie glanced at the paper. Sure enough, the brunette was standing behind the mayor's left shoulder.

"This was the one that really helped, though. It's at the fourth of July parade. She's standing behind him again, but look under the photo. The photographer listed the names of everyone on the stage.

"Karen Becker," Ellie read. "That's her?"

"That's her."

"Do you think Grace is right? Are they having an affair?"

"There's no way to tell," Shannon said. "She's known him for a while, judging by these pictures, and she's obviously gone to his house quite a bit over the last couple of months, but beyond that, we don't know anything."

"I should tell Grace," Ellie said, reaching for her friend. "She's going to want to go talk to this woman."

"Wait," her friend said, putting a hand on her arm. "I don't know how safe that would be. I know she thinks her brother-in-law killed his wife, but if he *is* having an affair with this Karen woman, then we have to consider her as a suspect, too."

"Why?"

"Ellie, come on. Are you really telling me that you can't think of a single reason why a man's mistress might want to kill his wife?"

"Well, if you put it that way," Ellie said, sighing. "I agree that Grace shouldn't go to question her alone. But what should we do?"

"We could go to the police," Shannon said. "Russell could look into this. I mean, we have evidence that they know each other, proof that she went over to his house alone, multiple times, and a name. That should be enough for him to at least question her on her involvement with the guy."

"But Grace is worried about Mayor Martin going after her, if he gets wind that someone's been talking to the police about his personal life. I don't want to put her in danger."

"Well, she's going to be in danger if she goes to talk to this lady on her own," her friend pointed out.

Ellie thought about it, then agreed reluctantly. "Okay, we can tell Russell. Grace seemed pretty determined to uncover all of this, and I don't think she'll listen to our concerns for her safety. But I'm still going to tell her after we tell the sheriff, so she can be on her toes."

"All right, I guess that's a good compromise," Shannon said. "Do you want to call him, or should I?"

"I'll do it. I want to see if he's made any progress with those jerks at Cheesaroni yet."

Shannon raised her eyebrows. The pizzeria manager realized that she hadn't had a chance to tell her friend about the vandalism yet. She gave her a quick summary while Sheriff Ward's number rang. When he answered, she put him on speaker phone and began to tell him all about her conversations with Grace Camper, and the amateur detective work that she and Shannon had done.

"Didn't I ask both of you to stay far away from all of this?" the sheriff asked when she had finished catching him up. He sounded caught between amusement and annoyance.

"Well, *she* approached *me*," Ellie said. "I didn't feel like I could turn her away, not when she's grieving the death of her sister."

"And all I did was go through some old newspapers," Shannon added. "I'm a grown woman, Russ. I know James wants you to keep me out of trouble, but honestly, this is what I enjoy doing."

Russell sighed, and Ellie could imagine him running his hands through his hair. "I'll look into it," he said. "We've got a few of our own leads, but I'll at least give your theory a once-over. That's all I can promise, though. Even if she was having some sort of an affair with the mayor, well, cheating on your spouse isn't illegal. Being immoral doesn't necessarily mean that either of them are killers."

With that, he hung up. Ellie and Shannon traded a look.

"He's not taking this seriously at all," the journalist said.

"To be fair, last time I tried to convince him someone was a murderer, I was completely wrong about it all and almost got myself killed," Ellie said. "I don't really blame him for having his doubts."

"Well, it may not bother *you*, but I'm tired of him thinking he can tell me what to do just because he's my brother-in-law and the sheriff. I've always wanted to be some sort of investigator, you know that. I love digging for the truth. I'm not the sort of woman that's going to be happy just sitting around here while a man does all of the work. Not to mention that I hate it when people don't take me seriously. Just because I'm not a fifty-year-old man with a gun, doesn't mean I don't know what I'm doing."

"What are you saying?" the pizzeria manager asked. "Should we go question this lady ourselves?"

"That's exactly what I'm saying," Shannon said with a grin. "Call up Grace, too. There's safety in numbers. If it turns out that Karen is the guilty one, well, she can't murder all of us."

CHAPTER FIFTEEN

G race was glad to hear the news that the woman in the photos had been identified. She was even happier when Shannon invited her to meet them at the car pool lot to go with them to talk to Karen Becker. It hadn't been hard to track down more information about her; she was a psychologist who lived in Kittiport, but had an office in Benton Harbor. She had office hours until five that evening; the perfect opportunity for the three women to go and talk to her.

They decided to wait and go see her as close to five as possible, figuring that the best time to catch her would be right after her last patient of the day left. They spent the few hours beforehand at the Pacelli house, making more no-bake cookies and going over the questions that they wanted to ask the woman. Even Nonna got involved, and it took Ellie a while to convince her grandmother that she had to stay home.

"Chances are, this Karen lady is perfectly nice," she said. "But if she does know something about Laura Martin's murder, then she might be dangerous, and we might have to run."

"And I'd just slow you down," the older woman said with a sigh. "I know you're right. I want to hear all about it when you get back. My granddaughter, solving murders. Who would have thought?"

Ellie, Shannon, and Grace got to the building that housed Karen Becker's office a good half an hour before five. The receptionist beckoned them over to the desk when they came in.

"Who are ya' here to see?" she drawled, her southern accent marking her as a non-local.

"Dr. Karen Becker," Ellie said.

The receptionist clicked a few times, then peered at them more closely. "She doesn't have any more appointments this evening. Are you sure y'all have the right day? What name is the appointment under?"

"We're actually here to see her about a personal matter."

"Well, she doesn't usually take walk-ins." The receptionist chewed on the end of her pen. "I'll have to send her a note. If she doesn't want to see you, you got to leave."

"Okay. Just... just tell her we're here to talk about Mayor Martin and his wife."

They waited anxiously as the woman behind the computer typed a message to her boss. After a few minutes, she looked over at them and sighed. "She says she'll see you, but it can't take long. She'll be with you in about ten minutes. Feel free to help yourself to coffee or tea and cookies while you wait."

The three women sat down, relieved that they had successfully crossed the first hurdle. All they really needed to know was if Karen had been having an affair with the mayor; Shannon thought that might be enough to get Russell to take them more seriously and question her. Ellie wasn't holding her breath that the woman would come out and admit to an affair, but with Grace along, she might just feel guilty enough to let something slip.

A door leading from the reception area opened up, and a man in a tweed suit walked out, followed by a brunette. "I'll see you next week. Don't forget to work on those breathing exercises we practiced." The woman was easily recognizable as the lady from the photos. She was smiling, but the expression faded when her gaze landed on Ellie, Shannon, and Grace.

"You three, come on back," she said.

They followed her to a comfortable office, with a plush love seat and a couple of armchairs. The walls were lined with bookshelves, and the warm scent of a vanilla candle pervaded the air. It didn't exactly seem like the den of a dangerous woman. Ellie felt herself relax.

"What can I do for the three of you?" the woman asked as she sat down at her desk. Her voice was cold.

"We're here to ask some questions about Mayor Martin," Shannon said calmly. "Specifically, what is your relationship with him? How well do you know him?"

Karen was opening her mouth to respond when Grace cut in.

"You're sleeping with him, aren't you?" she said in a voice high pitched with emotion. "I knew it. I knew he was cheating on Laura, but it took me this long to figure out with who."

"What in the world are you talking about?" the psychologist said, taken aback.

"I have pictures of you coming to his house, alone, every single week."

"I know this is hard for you, Grace," Ellie said. "But remember, we aren't here to accuse her of anything. We just need the truth, whatever it is."

"I am not, nor have I ever, been romantically involved with a married man," Karen said, her words taut with disapproval. "And I would appreciate it if all three of you would leave. I don't enjoy having accusations thrown at me in my own place of work. I shouldn't have agreed to see you at all."

"We aren't trying to throw accusations at you," Shannon said, casting an annoyed glance at Grace. "I'm a journalist. I have a column in the Kittiport newspaper. As I'm sure you know, Laura Martin's death has been big news in our little town. Some people think that her husband is the one that killed her. The pictures of you coming to his house on a regular basis will only feed rumors of an affair, which strengthens the position of those who think he's a killer. Being caught in an affair is as good a motive for murder as any, and a better motive than anyone else would have had. So if you're his friend, just tell me the truth about how you know him. It could save a lot of grief and trouble on his part."

Karen licked her lips, looking between them. "Does this stay off the record?"

"If you want," Shannon said.

"He wasn't having an affair. With anyone. We've been friends for years, and more recently, I've been acting as a therapist for couple's counseling sessions for him and his wife, may she rest in peace. I shouldn't even be telling you that much, but he does not deserve to have his name dragged through the mud. Please don't insinuate anything in your article that isn't true." She stood up to see them to the door, then paused mid-stride. Her eyes rested on Grace.

"What did you say your name was?"

"This is Grace Camper," Ellie said when the other woman made no move to introduce herself.

"Laura's sister?" Karen's eyes went wide. "I think you need to leave right now."

"But—"

"Leave, or I'm calling the police." She reached for the phone on her desk, but Grace stepped forward and yanked the cable out of the receiver.

"I was wondering if they'd said anything about me," she said. "I guess I got my answer."

"What are you talking about, Grace?" Shannon said.

"Laura's sister," Karen said, sitting back down in her seat heavily. "She served five years in prison for assault when she discovered that the man she had been seeing had a wife. She nearly killed the poor woman. I knew you were staying with them, but I didn't make the connection until now."

"What are you talking about?" Ellie asked, dumbfounded by the turn of events.

"If I had to guess, I'd say this is the woman that killed Laura Martin. Grace killed her own sister."

CHAPTER SIXTEEN

Ellie and Shannon both took a step back, trading a horrified glance. It didn't make sense. Grace had seemed so earnest in her search for her sister's killer.

"What did they say about me?" the sister asked, casually walking over to the outlet and unplugging the computer.

"They told me about your past. A history of unstable relationships. How you would obsess over each guy you went out with, then have a breakdown the moment he didn't meet your expectations." Karen wasn't looking at Grace as she spoke. Her eyes were on Ellie. The pizzeria manager stared back at her, still confused but beginning to realize that they had walked in to a bad situation.

"What else?" the woman asked, walking slowly around the desk to stand behind the psychologist. She leaned over her and delicately picked up a letter opener shaped like a dagger from Karen's desk. "Did Ambrose talk about me?"

"They told me you had gotten out of prison and were staying with them for a while, until you got your feet back under you." Karen paused. "I'm sorry, Grace, but could you please put that letter opener down? It's making me uncomfortable."

"I'm not going to hurt you, not unless those two make a break for the door, anyway. I need some sort of collateral. You see, I really don't want to go to prison again." She poked the psychologist in the shoulder with the blunted blade. "Continue. I want to know what they said."

"There isn't much else. Why don't *you* take a turn at talking, Grace? You could tell us a little bit about your life with them."

"What is there to say? I fell in love the day I moved in." Laura's sister sighed and leaned back against the wall. "Ambrose was so nice to me. I knew we could be together, just as soon as I found out a way to make Laura leave. I can't believe I thought he was having an affair with someone else — I guess that's what I get for eavesdropping. I kept hearing them mention some other woman, but that was just you, their therapist."

133

"So you fell in love with him, and wanted to get his wife out of the way?" Karen asked. She was still looking at Ellie, darting her eyes to something behind her right shoulder. The pizzeria manager began slowly turning her head, scared that if she made a sudden move, Grace would snap.

"I was prepared to wait," Grace said. "I knew that he loved me too, and he would leave her eventually."

"Then why did you kill her?" the psychologist asked. "She was your sister. I don't think you wanted to hurt her."

Ellie continued to turn her head, finally catching a glimpse of something out of the corner of her eye. There was a fire alarm on the wall beside the door behind her. She glanced back at Karen, who gave the slightest of nods.

"I didn't want to hurt her," Grace was saying. "You're right about that. Like I said, I was willing to wait. But then their relationship started getting better, and they began spending more time together." Her brows furrowed. "That must have been your doing. I decided to take matters into my own hands. I began doing little things to sabotage them. I switched the fake flowers for live ones. Laura's been allergic to pollen her whole life. She gets all stuffed up and blotchy, and it isn't very attractive. I thought that would drive Ambrose away, but it didn't work. He didn't seem to care. I had to up the ante. I began undercooking her meat during our meals together, I never washed any of the vegetables for her plate, I let the milk that she used for her coffee every morning sit out. Anything I could think of to make her sick. I grew up with her; I know just how horrible she gets when she doesn't feel well."

"You're the one that gave her food poisoning that day at the pizzeria!" Shannon exclaimed, speaking for the first time since Grace had shown her true colors.

The other woman nodded. "It must have been the chicken from the night before. Hers was barely cooked, and I set it on the counter for two hours before beginning to prepare the meal. I can't imagine how she didn't notice it. Or maybe she did notice it, because later that night she asked me to take a walk with her, down by the marina. She told me that she wanted me to move out. I just... I snapped."

"I'm sure it feels good to get all of this off your chest, Grace. How do you feel about everything that you've done?"

"Don't try your shrinky stuff with me — wait, what is that in your hand?"

Grace let the letter opener clatter to the floor as she grabbed Karen's arm. Ellie decided that was her signal; she lunged for the fire alarm and gave it a sharp pull. Immediately an earsplitting alarm started blaring and bright lights began flashing. Grace and Shannon both let out shrieks of shock, but Karen, who had been expecting it, used that moment to yank her arm out of Grace's grip and jump out of her chair. The two women scuffled, but now that Grace was unarmed, they were evenly matched.

Ellie was surprised when Shannon let out a shout and ran forward into the fray. Her friend had been frozen with fear the entire time, but finally seemed to have overcome it. The two women managed to restrain Grace in no time. Shannon used the phone cord that the other woman had ripped from the wall minutes before to bind her hands behind her back, and they forced her into the chair behind the desk. With both the journalist and the psychologist standing guard over her, Grace wasn't going anywhere.

"Call the police," Karen shouted over the noise of the alarm. "Tell them we have Laura Martin's killer — and a taped confession." She held up her hand and revealed what had caused Grace to panic the moment before the alarm went off; a palm sized voice recorder, with the red recording light still on.

EPILOGUE

T he street outside of the office building was chaotic. The fire department had responded to the alarm, and the truck was parked on the curb while volunteer firemen spoke to the local police. Grace had already been taken away, and Karen had turned in the voice recording at the same time. Each of the three women had been questioned, and though they were finally free to go, they were still standing in a huddle by the building.

"I can't believe all of that just happened," Shannon said. "We spent hours with her, and she seemed so normal. She was in your house, Ellie."

"I know." Ellie shuddered. "It doesn't seem real, does it? I never would have thought that she was the one that did it. She just didn't seem like a killer."

"I should have connected the dots sooner," Karen said. "After everything they told me about her, I still didn't guess that she was the one that killed Laura until I saw how she reacted in my office when she thought I had been having an affair with Ambrose."

"We should have listened to Russ and kept out noses out of it." The journalist sighed. "Why is my brother-in-law always right?"

"I don't know if he's *always* right," Ellie said. "He must be wrong sometimes. It's just that we're wrong a lot more often." She winced at the thought of what he would say when he heard of this latest fiasco. How did she always manage to end up in such deep water? Thinking back over the past few days, she tried to see the signs that she was dealing with a madwoman, but couldn't.

"Sorry, by the way," Shannon said, turning to Karen. "It was completely our fault for dragging you into all of this. If we had known —"

"Don't worry about it. No one got hurt, after all, and we did manage to send a killer to prison."

"It was quick thinking, using that voice recorder."

"You'd be surprised how many times I've gotten death threats. I deal with a lot of people who have self-control issues, and if I ever had to defend myself, I'd need some sort of proof on my side. I've gotten pretty good at using that thing without anyone noticing."

"Well, still... sorry." Shannon sighed and glanced up at the sky. "It looks like it might rain soon. We should probably get going, Ellie. I just know that Russell is going to be calling us as soon as he hears about this. I want to tell James what happened first. He never likes hearing things secondhand from the sheriff."

"All right. I need to get back to Nonna and tell her what happened as well. I *did* promise her I'd tell her all about it, though she probably isn't expecting such an exciting story."

They said their goodbyes to Karen, waved to the somewhat befuddled police officers — the one that had interviewed them had seemed very impressed that three women had managed to subdue a killer on their own — and got into Ellie's car. As she put it into gear, the pizzeria manager turned to look at her friend. Their gazes met, and they both grinned. Neither of them wanted to repeat the experience any time soon, but they weren't exactly complaining, either. They hadn't exactly solved the mystery, but still, they had caught a murderer, and there was something to be said for that.

98772826R00079

Made in the USA
Lexington, KY
10 September 2018